I believe this history more than the few sentences i in most breed books. Though I the family's request, avoided speculation, I hope that this narrative humanizes the story. (Some of the photos that illustrate it are mine; as far as I know and believe, the others are in the public domain and beyond copyright.)

All that being said, this work is copyrighted. All rights are reserved under the Pan-American and International Copyright Conventions. This book may not be reproduced in whole or in part, in any form or by any means, electronic or mechanical, including any information storage or retrieval system now known or hereafter invented or developed, without written permission from the copyright holder.

Introduction

He was a gash an' faithful tyke,
As ever lap a sleugh or dyke,
His honest, sonsie, baws'nt face,
Ay gat him friends in like place.

⁓ These lines of Robert Burns' description
of his Border Collie, Luath, in *Twa Dogs: a Tale*
might as well be of a Westie

This book was inspired by my Scottish heritage: I am a member of the Clan MacCallum-Malcolm, and one of our "clancestors," Col. Edward Donald Malcolm, developed and named the breed known as the West Highland White Terrier.

The clan seat is at Duntrune, an ancient castle that dates to the twelfth century; the curtain wall was added in the thirteenth, and the tower house – according to the Historic Houses Association, the oldest continuously occupied castle on the Scottish mainland – is from the seventeenth century. It sits on the north side of Loch Crinan and across from the village of Crinan in Argyll, a county in the Scottish Highlands.

Just as I couldn't resist writing a few pages about how we came to welcome Wee Dram into our home, I think Col. Malcolm's commitment and devotion merits more than the one or two paragraphs his and his dogs' story usually gets in breed books. I hope you enjoy this version of the story every MacCallum and Malcolm should know.

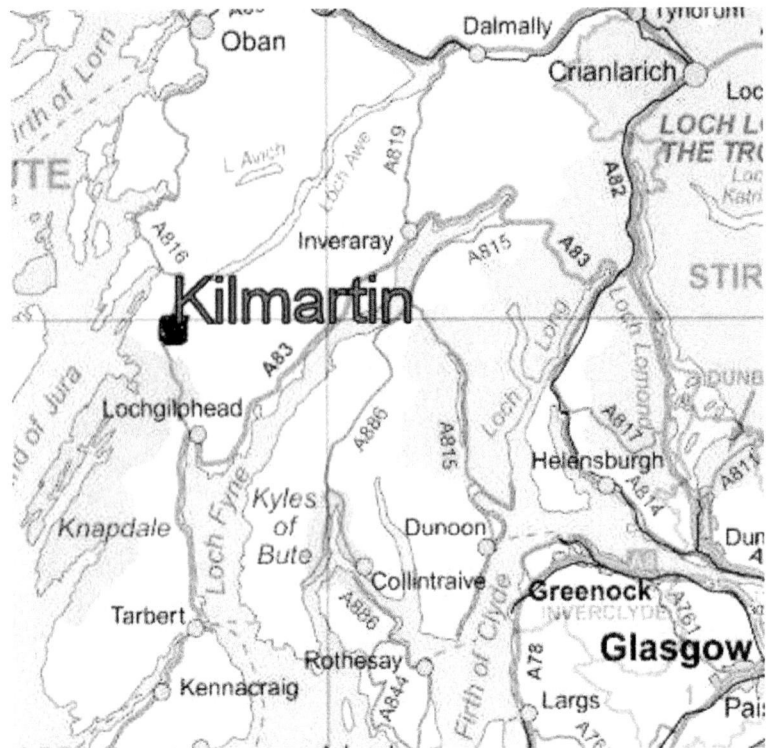

Kilmartin is the nearest town to Duntrune. The Clan MacCallum-Malcolm seat is on the mainland, overlooking the Sound of Jura.

The Kilmartin Glen is a significant archaeological site, with one of the most significant concentrations of Neolithic and Bronze Age remains in Scotland; there are more than 800 ancient monuments within six miles of the village. The Kilmartin Museum (**www.Kilmartin.org**) houses some finds, and interprets the landscape.

Nearby, the Kilmartin Church is the site of seventy-nine early Christian and medieval carved gravestones. If you claim MacCallum or Malcolm ancestry, this is an excellent place to begin or continue your research.

The author took this photo of the Kilmartin Church graveyard.

This view of the Kilmartin Glen is from the area just south of the museum.

This is the author's 2009 photo of the Kilmartin House Museum, which is now under expansion!

Here's the Kilmartin Parish Church (a congregation of the Church of Scotland), visited in 2009 after the Gathering of the Clans in Edinburgh.

It's All About the Little White Dog

The story begins even earlier than around 1600 or so, when James I of England (James VI of Scotland) sent for a dozen or so white "earth dogges" from Argyleshire to give as gifts to the King of France. Alas, there are no definitive records of such dogs prior to James' gift, but they must've been well-known and highly thought of to be fit for a gift from one head of state to another.

We know that throughout the seventeenth century, farmers in the Highlands bred short-legged, flat-ribbed terriers for hunting small game and vermin. Current thinking is that these dogs originated on Skye centuries ago, but nobody knows for *sure*.

Edward Donald Malcolm was born on 13 November, 1837, the third son of John Malcolm, the 14th Laird of Poltalloch, and Isabella Harriet Wingfield. He married Australian-born Isabella Wyld-Brown on July 17, 1867 after graduating as a lieutenant from the Royal Military Academy at Woolwich.

It took him another sixteen years to make colonel, and that wasn't until two years after he'd been made a Companion in the Order of the Bath. His postings had been worldwide: they'd been stationed in India, in China, in Canada. He retired from the service in 1894 He died on March 20, 1930, and in the meantime, developed and named the breed we now know as West Highland White Terriers – Westies.

In an undated interview, Col. Edward Donald Malcolm explained, "I want my readers to understand this, not to think of a Highland fox cairn [one of the names Westies used to go by; not today's fox terrier] as if it were an English fox earth dog in sand, nor of badger work as if it were a question of locating the badger and then digging him out.

"No, the badger makes his home amongst rocks, the small ones perhaps two or three tons in weight, and probably he has his hinner end against one of three or four hundred tons. There's no digging him out, and, moreover, the passages between the rocks must be taken as they are, no scratching them a little wider."

The breed we know today as the West Highland White Terrier, has a long story, one to which Malcolm contributed significantly. As we can piece it together from public records, here is the history of this marvelous little dog.

By the time Malcolm married Isabella, his oldest brother, John Wingfield Malcolm, had been married for six years. The family's second son, Leonard Neill, had died in Russia at the age of nineteen, as a lieutenant with the Rifle Brigade in the Battle of Inkerman. His mother had survived Leonard's death by only four years. His sister, another Isabella, was young, and unmarried herself; she would marry Alfred Gathorne-Hardy before too much longer.

Edward Malcolm and his brother John were not quite about alone in their acceptance of the lighter-colored ones ... but most farmers and hunters – and not just locally – destroyed them at birth, believing them to be "weak."

Edward and John knew from their father's and grandfather's experience that their light-colored dogs were just as sturdy and ferocious as the reds, and as the darker ones. They didn't go out of their way to get white or sand-colored dogs, but they kept those that were whelped, and trained them up with the others. They were certainly easier to see in the dim light of early morning and late evening, and in the dappled light of sparse woods and fields.

In response to Thomson Gray's mention of the Poltalloch Terrier, in *Dogs of Scotland*, published in 1887, Col. Malcolm contacted the author.

"The Poltalloch terriers still exist in the Poltalloch Kennels," he wrote, "and I hope that your recognition of them may make it more possible to keep them up. They are not invariably white, but run between creamy white and sandy.

"A good one at his best looks like a handsome deerhound reduced in some marvelous way. They are gameness itself, and terrible poachers. They love above all things to get away with a young retriever, and run him forever, teaching him everything he ought not to know.

"As for wisdom, make one your friend and he will know everything and do it. I have known one whose usual amusement was rat-killing, and who never retrieved – never went into a hole in tender ice to bring out a wild duck – because, I suppose, he thought it a shame to waste it when his master had shot it.

"This chap had a great friend, a mastiff bitch, and he used to swim along water-rat infested streams, and she, applying her nose to the landward hole, would snort a rat out of his wits into the water, and into the terrier's jaws, where the terrier, silently swimming, was keeping pace with his friend. They are said in the kennels to have a trick of suddenly turning upon one of the rats' number and putting it to death, and when they do this they leave little mark of their work, as they eat their victim.

"They are kept for work – fox and otter hunting. They have consequently been kept small, and without the power which seems to be of such value on the show bench. This could easily be got by feeding up, but then the dogs would be of no use in the fox cairns.

"As it is, they often push in between rocks they cannot escape from, and so the best get lost."

Malcolm readily admitted that although after 1860, he focused his breeding program on light-colored and white dogs, he did not create them. His father and grandfather both kept them, along with dogs of other colors; none of them subscribed to the idea that the lighter-colored dogs, and especially the white ones, were in any way inferior.

Years earlier, one of Malcolm's father's dogs had gotten lost in a cairn. The keepers went there daily, hoping against hope. At last one day a pair of bright eyes were seen at the bottom of a hole. They did not disappear when the dog's name was called, so ....

"Quite a brilliant idea seized one of the keepers," Malcolm told the story in an interview. "The dog evidently could not get up on his own, so a rabbit skin was folded into a small parcel round a stone and let down by a string. The dog at once seized the situation, and the skin, held on, was drawn up, and fainted on reaching the mouth of the hole. He was carried home tenderly and nursed; he recovered."

The Malcolms – a clan that still includes MacCallums, though Dugald MacCallum changed his name in 1779, after inheriting Malcolm estates – took it for granted that the little white dogs had been abundant in

Scotland since at least the days of King James the Sixth of Scotland.

When he became James the First of England in 1603, he asked for a dozen or so "little white earth dogges" from Argyleshire in Scotland, to give as a gift to the King of France. It seems obvious that these were the forerunners of the dog that Poltalloch Kennels was breeding now.

(Poltalloch House – which some knew as Callton Mor – had only been finished a few years earlier, in 1853. Outside, the stone was very finely dressed. Ashlar, people called that style of masonry. L-shaped and a particularly nice shade of golden buff, the place was designed by William Burn.)

Back in 'sixty, one of Malcolm's hunts had been going well, until both the first and second fields had heard a cry that stopped them in their tracks. Something had gone very wrong.

As it turned out, it wasn't a man or a horse that had gone down. It was one of Malcolm's dogs, a light brown Cairn, one of his favorites. Today, some versions of the story say it was a guest who'd shot the dog, and some say it was Malcolm himself; we may never know. What we do know is what he did to keep such an accident from happening again.

He built a kennel of white terriers, no more to resemble, even slightly, otters or badgers or foxes. There were arguments against that course. "You know, even if the white dogs are sturdy enough," people said, "by the time they go to ground, they're not white dogs anymore."

But the white dogs' coats were hard; a brisk shake and they were free of most of the dirt – and the terriers would certainly shake, just to make sure their prey was well killed.

The first generation of light-colored dogs had been sandy, but they'd had the pricked ears; by 1897 they were almost completely white. One question that faced Malcolm was whether to breed these dogs to Dr. Flaxman's bitch.

Dr. Americ Edwin Flaxman began to experiment with dog breeding on the advice of his tutor, Professor Thomas Huxley. After settling in Fife in the early 1880s, Flaxman was interested for some time in breeding trotters, and was president of the Trotting Union of Scotland. He liked breeding dogs even better than breeding horses, though, and worked with many breeds, including Pyrenean wolfhounds, Dalmatians, Yorkshire Terriers ... and Scottish Terriers. One of his Scottie bitches, Splinter II, was dark, but threw at least one white pup in every litter, no matter the sire.

Although he drowned about two dozen white puppies before it occurred to him that he might make something of the white ones, he finally wondered whether they might represent the original color of the stock. After ten years of breeding to the light-colored dogs, Flaxman achieved white Scotties.

Today, Scotties' colors range from dark grey to the most familiar pure black, as well as from straw to nearly white; they can be brindled as well. And even today, the record is not definite as to whether or not Malcolm bred any of his dogs to Flaxman's white-throwing bitch.

Flaxman's Pittenweems, though Splinter II was throwing white pups, were still Scottish Terriers. It wasn't a question of the quality of the pedigrees. Flaxman's dogs were all decent, and the bitch in question came from good lines. But they didn't really have the same look, save for their color. The Scotties were (and are) longer of muzzle, longer of body, and more bowlegged than the dogs Malcolm was breeding.

Malcolm's gamekeeper, William Young, had seen the light colored dogs do just as well as any other. But ... with their own dogs, the Malcolms knew the whole line, knew its performance and how each dog developed. With another man's bitch, one could know the pedigree, but not the dogs themselves.

It was tricky enough with one's own dogs to breed for color without sacrificing anything else. Bringing in the unknown with another man's bitch – or stud, for that matter – made the whole enterprise more complicated. Nasty surprises could lay in wait a generation or two down the line.

New blood was certainly required, but George Campbell, the Duke of Argyll, had a fine kennel and the same need to crossbreed. And there were farmers thereabouts who had good dogs of their own. Flaxman's bitch was never Malcolm's only choice.

Publicly establishing, and maintaining, the distinction between Scottish Terriers and the West Highland Whites was important. Malcolm could not tolerate his dogs being considered a sub-variety, and breeding to Flaxman's bitch would have condemned them to that fate.

Malcolm's 'keeper, Young, had sent a telegram from a show in Edinburgh, after his dogs had outshone Flaxman's in the Poltalloch Terrier class. (Of course it was significant that the class was called Poltalloch, not Pittenweem.) "We busted Flaxman's guts!" Young wired.

In light of these factors, it's this author's guess that Malcolm did not breed his dogs with Flaxman's – but we may never know for sure.

These Pittenweems (L-R, Miss Tich, Nipper, and Bessie) were photographed in 1899.

Dr. Flaxman is pictured here, in about 1907, with some of his Pittenweems.

Sir Ian with a few of his Poltalloch Terriers.

Head Keeper William Young (l) and his son Alexander, hunting with Poltalloch Terriers.

Provost Colin Young, judging Westies at an LKA show in 1908.

Col. Malcolm is featured on this logo for Westie Day, observed since 2007. The date of March 20th was chosen to commemorate Col. Malcolm's death.

Confronting fierce prey, like this badger, was a routine part of a Westie's workday.

Four of Mrs. Cameron-Head's dogs from Inverailort, in about 1909.

The first champion in the breed was Morven, owned by Colin Young. However, because he was originally registered as a Scottish Terrier, Morven's first win, at seven months old, didn't count toward his championship as a Westie.

More of Poltalloch Kennels' dogs.

"These terriers must be shown in working clothes. Only a bit tidied up, washed and brushed and in possession of their valuable undercoat."

So Edward Donald Malcolm insisted to the end of his life, and for some time his view prevailed. As the little white dogs were more widely accepted, there was more and more competition, friendly for the most part, among the Eighth Duke, Dr. Flaxman, and Col. Malcolm. Generally, Malcolm's dogs were favored, perhaps because he was himself a hunter and took an active part in developing his dogs' pedigrees.

A Mrs. Cameron-Head bred little white dogs, too: the Drynochs, which were small enough to go to earth, but strong enough to fight the quarry when they got there. Christian Cameron was a headstrong woman who had been running her family's estate at Inverailort since her father Duncan's death in 1875. She was married to retired Army Captain James Head, and the mother of eleven-year-old twins, Frances and Christian.

She was a member of the English West Highland White Terrier Club as well as the Scottish. The breed's name had only recently been changed, so Poltallochs, Pittenweems, Roseneaths ... and Drynochs ... were no more. By 1908 (1909 in the U.S.), the little white dogs – excepting, of course, the white Scotties - were all known as Westies.

It wasn't necessary for Malcolm's dogs to go farther than to Edinburgh, or Glasgow, for shows. Flaxman had entered two dogs, Regina and Billy, in the London show at the Crystal Palace in 1899. Neither of them won; the champion white Scottish Terrier was from Captain Keene's dogs, White Victor and White Heather. Nothing to do with Westies, though: these, like Flaxman's dogs, were Scotties bred white.

At that time there was still very little distinction among the Scottish Terriers. Since the show in Birmingham in 1860, there'd been just two breeds recognized: Dandie Dinmonts and Skyes, with the latter category including the Scotties, the Cairns, the Poltallochs, Pittenweems, Roseneaths, and the silky-eared Skyes.

The problem was that, whether or how it was true or not, people believed that all the Highland terriers had originally come from Skye, and might be the progeny of a cross from a poodle brought from Spain.

But the Dandies had been a distinct breed since the turn of the eighteenth century, and when Sir Walter Scott, in his novel *Guy Mannering*, published in 1829, described a pack of them as belonging to a character called Dandie Dinmont, their name was fixed. That left the other dogs to be called Skye Terriers, no matter how distinctly they were being bred by the turn of the twentieth century.

All that was changing, though. Malcolm himself had begun the change: although his line of dogs was consistently judged the best, he did not want credit, and insisted on calling them West Highland White Terriers rather than Poltallochs. It was a specific enough name to identify them – to distinguish them from Scottish Terriers, even the white ones – and saluted their origins in the rugged Highlands, which their character tended to match.

Niall Campbell, the Tenth Duke of Argyll, formed the first breed club in 1904, and when it faded, the Countess of Aberdeen – ironic, perhaps, given that the Scotties were also known as Aberdeen Terriers – founded another, in England, the following year. Malcolm succeeded her as the club's president, a responsibility he took very seriously.

It was not surprising that Niall Campbell's club did not last. The Duke was eccentric, and many found his habits – especially of bursting into song, and, for example, offering Italian arias without warning – hard to take. For the most part, dog fanciers were sensible folk, and those used to terriers tended to be especially sensible, to balance their dogs' occasional mania. The Duke, though he maintained his grandfather's kennels, was, by all accounts, not well suited to working with the little white dogs now known as Westies.

The Countess of Aberdeen revived the club, and though they were still in some disagreement about distinguishing the breeds from one another, Malcolm accepted the vice-presidency and succeeded the Countess as head of the club when her term ended.

On the one hand, he appreciated that shows – well established since 1860 – brought fine dogs to the attention of the public, and assured their place in Scottish life. On the other, the shows seemed to be promoting changes in the breeds, and not just the Westies.

"There is beginning to be an undue regard for weight, and what they call strength," he'd say for the record. "And for grooming, which just means brushing out all the long hair to gratify the judge. One might as well judge of Sandow's strength, not by his performances, but by the kind of wax he puts on his moustache!"

(Eugen Sandow was a widely famous "bodybuilder" who performed all over Europe. At some shows, he lifted a full-grown horse over his head.)

"Not that the coat's not important," Malcolm would say, when he was interviewed or (often) called upon to speak as the greatest authority on the subject of West Highland White Terriers. ""The outer coat should be very soft on the forehead and get gradually harder towards the haunches."

Having a "harsh" coat made sense given the dogs' work, and was beginning to be popular as a standard, but it was easy to fake. Anturic acid bath salts were a well-advertised and thus popular cure for gout – and for sciatica, and rheumatism, and lumbago as well. The salts certainly had a "harshening" effect on human and canine hair.

"The outer coat shouldn't be long in the fancy show sense. It just needs to be long enough to cover the real coat, and keep it dry, so that a good shake or two will throw off most of the water. The undercoat, of course, has to be thick and naturally oily enough for the dog to swim through a fair sized river and not get wet.

"And of course he has to be able to sit out through a drenching rain guarding something without being any the worse. But do the judges look at the undercoat? I've never seen one do it, even though for the working terrier it is most important."

"Dogs," Malcolm said, "should not weigh more than one stone and four, and bitches not more than one stone and two." Eighteen pounds was the most he thought any Westie should weigh, with the bitches being lighter by a couple of pounds.

"And they should earn their living," he said. "They ought not be lap dogs, and most of them know that."

In 1910, the Kennel Club* settled the controversy about what to call Mrs. Campbell's dogs. She wanted to call them West Highland Terriers, leaving off 'white' because they weren't. The Kennel Club advised her to call them Cairn Terriers instead. And because the KC recognized them by that name, there wasn't much she could do about it.

---

* The Kennel Club, abbreviated KC, is the original, English one. All others are distinguished from it with additional initials: the American Kennel Club is the AKC, the Scottish Kennel Club is the SKC, and so on.

She argued with Sir Alexander Clyde about it; he was the Secretary of the Skye and Clydesdale Club. She argued the point with James Porritt, the Secretary of the Skye Club in England, too. But show categories were still in flux, and at the Inverness show she had to list her dogs as Skyes. Instead of listing them as 'Cairns or short-haired Skyes,'- she wanted to list them as 'prick-eared Skyes' - Mrs. Campbell and her friend Mary Hawke entered them in the Skye class, without any modification.

The judge disqualified them as being in the wrong class. She huffed about it, agreeing that they didn't match the Skye standard at all; this was, of course, exactly her point. Cairns were *not* Skye Terriers. Scottish Terriers were *not* Skye Terriers. And none of them were West Highland Whites.

The Skye Terrier clubs also complained to the KC, and said dogs shouldn't be listed as Skyes when they didn't meet the standard. The KC could hardly disagree with that, but of course they had to discuss it, so it would seem like their own idea. Their own idea was to begin a separate register for Cairns, which they did in May of 1910.

But there were some who continued to breed Cairns with Westies. It was still the case in the U.S. that both breeds could be registered from the same litter. Westies were gaining popularity in the States, but the identity confusion was unresolved. The breed had been recognized in the U.K. in 1907, but was still occasionally conflated with others.

With recognition of the breed, the KC's stud book began listing Westies in 1907, but it wasn't until the next year that the book showed any championship certificates awarded. Nine championships were conferred, and five of them went to Provost Colin Young's dog, Champion Morven; his offspring Cromar Snowflake, owned by the Countess of Aberdeen, was also a winner. Another of her dogs, Oronsay, finished his championship, too.

(It wasn't particularly suspicious that the breeders who gave the most support to the Clubs and shows were winning the prizes early on. They were, at first, the only ones breeding significant dogs)

In the U.S., the American Kennel Club stud books were listing Westies as Roseneath Terriers until 1910, and all five of the first-registered dogs were imported. An English dog, Clonmel Cream of the Skyes, known simply as Cream of the Skyes in the States, was America's first Westie to win his championship.

An American woman, a Mrs. Bacon, thought hers might be the first Westie brought over: White King, whelped in 1907, was one of C.F. Thompson's dogs. But Robert Goelet also claimed to have taken the first Westies over: Kiltie and Rumpus Glenmohr, in 1907.

None of the first dogs to move to America were Malcolm's, but he is nevertheless due some credit. It was true that he didn't really want to be heralded as the father of the breed, but his family's name will forever be associated with its development.

Isabella Wyld-Brown Malcolm died in 1927, at the age of eighty-one, leaving Col. Malcolm a widower at the age of eighty-eight. He joined her in death on March 20, 1930, at the age of ninety-two - knowing that his belovéd Westies' popularity was growing all over the world.

By 2010, Westies were the third most popular breed in the United Kingdom, and in the U.S., the thirty-fourth most popular breed. Malcolm did not live to see them win at Crufts or Westminster, but win at those most prestigious shows they have. They continue to be hardy dogs, despite Malcolm's worries that the show judges' demands would result in breeding away the very characteristics that made them the "earth dogges" they were born to be.

The children of Edward Donald Malcolm and Isabella Wyld Brown:
    Sir Ian Zachary Malcolm, b 1868
    Major-General Sir Neill Malcolm b 1869
    Margaret Emily Malcolm, b 1870
    Wingfield Malcolm, b 1872 d young
    George Harold Malcolm, b 1875
    Maurice de Wiveleslie Malcolm, b 1877
    William Alastair Malcolm, b 1881
    Dorothy Isabel Malcolm, b 1883

Robin Neill Lochnell Malcolm, the 19th Laird of Poltalloch, is Chief of Clan MacCallum-Malcolm, and lives at Duntrune. His father was George Ian Malcolm, the 18th Laid, and his grandfather was the 17th Laird Ian Zachary Malcolm, first son of Edward Donald Malcolm.

Poltalloch House in its heyday.

The author's composite photo of Duntrune Castle today.

A Chronological Overview of Events in the Westie's Development

1859

England's first-ever dog show was held in Newcastle-on-Tyne; only pointers and setters were shown. Later in the year, a second show was held in Birmingham, and spaniels were invited.

1860

The Birmingham show added hounds to the list. (The Birmingham show is still held, now in May of each year, and is about three times the size of Westminster, showing more than ten thousand dogs.)

1874

The first [English] Kennel Club stud book is published, and includes rules for the conduct of shows, as well as a calendar of events.

The first American dog show is held in Chicago, on June 4th – featuring only pointers and setters, for those were the dogs the organizers owned. A second American show was held in Oswego, New York, a few weeks later – but as there were only two entries, it was canceled.

However, in October, in Mineola, New York (on Long Island), a third show was held, and followed the [English] Kennel Club rules. At another October show, this one in Memphis, Tennessee, the first-ever American Best in Show award was given.

1877

The Westminster Show was founded, showing only sporting dogs. The show was wildly successful, and its length was extended from three days to four. The fourth day's gate was donated to the ASPCA.

1884

The American Kennel Club was formed in Philadelphia.

1897

A dog show in Glasgow was the first to include a Terrier group.

1904

The Scottish Kennel Club show in Edinburgh also included a Terrier group.

1905

Ch[ampion] Morven is the first Westie to finish his championship. He won his first title at seven months, but because he'd been registered as a Scottish Terrier, that win did not count toward his championship as a West Highland White Terrier.

1906

Westies are shown for the first time in American shows – as Roseneath Terriers.

1907

The first Crufts Show to recognize Westies was held in London.

1909

The AKC's fifteen-point championship rules were formed, and on the 31st of May, the name Roseneath

Terriers was officially changed to West Highland White Terriers. In the same year, the Canadian Kennel Club recognized Westies as a breed.

Just for the record, at about that time, a Model T Ford cost around $825 – and people were paying between $1,000 and $5,000 for purebred dogs.

1920

The AKC started sanctioning shows. (See below for the Westie's breed standard.)

1924

The two categories of Sporting and Non-Sporting dogs were split into five: Sporting (including Hounds), Terrier, Toy, Non-Sporting, and Working (including Herding). Today, in the U.S. and Canada, the Hounds and Herders have their own classification, so there are seven groups. Westies are in the Terrier Group.

Whether or not you are interested in dog shows, their evolution has been significant in the development, identification, and recognition of the various breeds. We have come a long way since the day when the wide-ranging types of terriers in Scotland were called anything from Skyes to fox-hounds; now we know the breeds from one another, and can take care that they are not bred too far from their original purposes.

More and more dog-oriented organizations and members of the public are standing against puppy mills and the "backyard breeders" who supply them. More and more people understand that buying puppies from pet stores only contributes to the breeding-for-profit-alone that puts so many dogs at risk and in misery.

The AKC recognizes Breeders of Merit, who adhere to strict standards. In addition to belonging to an AKC club, they must be involved with AKC events for at least five years, and have earned AKC Conformation, Performance, or Companion titles on at least four dogs from ACK-registered litters they bred or co-bred.

They must also certify that appropriate health screens (as recommended by the breed's parent club) are performed on their breeding stock, and demonstrate a commitment to ensuring that all of the puppies they produce are registered with the AKC.

(Pups that will not be shown can be registered as "limited," which means that any offspring they produce will not be eligible for registration, and the dog itself will not be eligible for shows. This is an appropriate choice if you're going to spay or neuter your purebred puppy.)

Additional ways that breeders will work with puppies include Dr. Carmen Battaglia's adrenal stimulation process, also called early neurological stimulation (ENS). This involves a sequential series of seconds-long tactile stimulations that have been shown to improve a pup's cardiovascular and immune systems, and improve its ability to handle stress. It's also common to play recordings of various sounds – traffic noise, other animals, household noises, and, in our pup's case, bagpipe music! – to desensitize the puppies so that these sounds will later be familiar.

Reputable breeders will not only have clean, airy, and spacious quarters for their dogs, they will also welcome your visit(s) and your questions. They will want to know something about you, too, about your attitudes toward pets, the time you have to spend with them, your willingness to train your dog or bitch, and where you will keep your dog(s), among other things.

Good breeders put an enormous amount of time and energy – not to mention money – into their dogs. Sleeping beside the whelping box when a litter is due is not uncommon, and neither are several-hour-long deliveries; sometimes, a bitch requires a C-section.

Many breeders choose to keep the puppies for twelve weeks rather than eight, just to make sure they get the right start in life. If you're looking for a purebred puppy, you need to look very carefully at the breeder you're considering – and be prepared for him or her to look very carefully at you, too!

If a purebred dog is not on your must-have list, then consider getting your canine companion from a local shelter or from an independent rescue group. Remember that for various reasons, purebreds – usually older dogs – are sometimes available from shelters and rescue groups.

You can find rescue groups in most states, and you can check with **WestieRescue.com** and/or **WestieClubAmerica.com** to find rescue opportunities where you live.

The American Kennel Club's Standard for the Westie

This breed standard, taken from the AKC website, was approved 13 December of 1988 and effective from 1 February 1989.

General Appearance: The West Highland White Terrier is a small, game, well-balanced hardy looking terrier, exhibiting good showmanship, possessed with no small amount of self-esteem, strongly built, deep in chest and back ribs, with a straight back and powerful hindquarters on muscular legs, and exhibiting in marked degree a great combination of strength and activity. The coat is about two inches long, white in color, hard, with plenty of soft undercoat. The dog should be neatly presented, the longer coat on the back and sides, trimmed to blend into the shorter neck and shoulder coat. Considerable hair is left around the head to act as a frame for the face to yield a typical Westie expression.

Size, Proportion, Substance: The ideal *size* is eleven inches at the withers for dogs and ten inches for bitches. A slight deviation is acceptable. The Westie is a compact dog, with good balance and *substance*. The body between the withers and the root of the tail is slightly shorter than the height at the withers. Short-coupled and well boned. Faults - Over or under height limits. Fine boned.

Head: Shaped to present a round appearance from the front. Should be in proportion to the body. *Expression* - Piercing, inquisitive, pert.

Eyes - Widely set apart, medium in size, almond shaped, dark brown in color, deep set, sharp and intelligent. Looking from under heavy eyebrows, they give a piercing look. Eye rims are black. Faults - Small, full or light colored eyes.

Ears - Small, carried tightly erect, set wide apart, on the top outer edge of the skull. They terminate in a sharp point, and must never be cropped. The hair on the ears is trimmed short and is smooth and velvety, free of fringe at the tips. Black skin pigmentation is preferred. Faults - Round-pointed, broad, large, ears set closely together, not held tightly erect, or placed too low on the side of the head.

Skull - Broad, slightly longer than the muzzle. not flat on top but slightly domed between the ears. It gradually tapers to the eyes. There is a defined stop, eyebrows are heavy. Faults - Long or narrow skull.

Muzzle - Blunt, slightly shorter than the skull, powerful and gradually tapering to the nose, which is large and black. The jaws are level and powerful. Lip pigment is black. Faults - Muzzle longer than skull. Nose color other than black.

Bite - The teeth are large for the size of the dog. There must be six incisor teeth between the canines of both lower and upper jaws. An occasional missing premolar is acceptable. A tight scissors bite with upper incisors slightly overlapping the lower incisors or level mouth is equally acceptable. Faults - Teeth defective or misaligned. Any incisors missing or several premolars missing. Teeth overshot or undershot.

Neck, Topline, Body: *Neck* - Muscular and well set on sloping shoulders. The length of neck should be in proportion to the remainder of the dog. Faults - Neck too long or too short.

Topline - Flat and level, both standing and moving. Faults - High rear, any deviation from above.

Body - Compact and of good substance. Ribs deep and well arched in the upper half of rib, extending at least to the elbows, and presenting a flattish side appearance. Back ribs of considerable depth, and distance from last rib to upper thigh as short as compatible with free movement of the body. Chest very deep and extending to the elbows, with breadth in proportion to the size of the dog. Loin short, broad and strong. Faults - Back weak, either too long or too short. Barrel ribs, ribs above elbows.

Tail - Relatively short, with good substance, and shaped like a carrot. When standing erect it is never extended above the top of the skull. It is covered with hard hair without feather, as straight as possible, carried gaily but not curled over the back. The tail is set on high enough so that the spine does not slope down to it. The tail is never docked. Faults - Set too low, long, thin, carried at half-mast, or curled over back.

Forequarters:

Angulation, Shoulders - Shoulder blades are well laid back and well knit at the backbone. The shoulder blade should attach to an upper arm of moderate length, and sufficient angle to allow for definite body overhang. Faults - Steep or loaded shoulders. Upper arm too short or too straight.

Legs - Forelegs are muscular and well boned. relatively short, but with sufficient length to set the dog up so as not to be too close to the ground. The legs are reasonably straight, and thickly covered with short hard hair. They are set in under the shoulder blades with definite body overhang before them. Height from elbow to withers and elbow to ground should be approximately the same. Faults - Out at elbows. Light bone, fiddle-front.

Feet - Forefeet are larger than the hind ones, are round, proportionate in size, strong, thickly padded; they may properly be turned out slightly. Dewclaws may be removed. Black pigmentation is most desirable on pads of all feet and nails, although nails may lose coloration in older dogs.

Hindquarters:

Angulation - Thighs are very muscular, well angulated, not set wide apart, with hock well bent, short, and parallel when viewed from the rear. Legs - Rear legs are muscular and relatively short and sinewy. Faults - Weak hocks, long hocks, lack of angulation. Cowhocks.

Feet - Hind feet are smaller than front feet, and are thickly padded. Dewclaws may be removed.

Coat: Very important and seldom seen to perfection. Must be double-coated. The head is shaped by plucking the hair, to present the round appearance. The outer coat consists of straight hard white hair, about two inches long, with shorter coat on neck and shoulders, properly blended and trimmed to blend shorter areas into furnishings, which are longer on stomach and legs. The ideal coat is hard, straight and white, but a hard straight coat which may have some wheaten tipping is preferable to a white fluffy or soft coat. Furnishings may be somewhat softer and longer but should never give the appearance of fluff. Faults - Soft coat. Any silkiness or tendency to curl. Any open or single coat, or one which is too short.

Color: The color is white, as defined by the breed's name. Faults - Any coat color other than white. Heavy wheaten color.

Gait: Free, straight and easy all around. It is a distinctive gait, not stilted, but powerful, with reach and drive. In front the leg is freely extended forward by the shoulder. When seen from the front the legs do not move square, but tend to move toward the center of gravity. The hind movement is free, strong and fairly close. The hocks are freely flexed and drawn close under the body, so that when moving off the foot the body is thrown or pushed forward with some force. Overall ability to move is usually best evaluated from the side, and topline remains level. Faults - Lack of reach in front, and/or drive behind. Stiff, stilted or too wide movement.

Temperament: Alert, gay, courageous and self-reliant, but friendly. Faults - Excess timidity or excess pugnacity.

Of course, not all Westies are show dogs; and only those which have not been spayed or neutered can participate in conformation events. This is because those events – the Westminster and Eukanuba and other shows you see televised, for instance – are to determine which animals best represent the breed and are best suited to maintain and improve it through breeding. However, the ACK has in recent years opened other events, such as obedience, rally, and agility, to unregistered purebreds and mixed breeds.

In most areas, there are dog parks, and dog clubs who host events that are open to any breed or mixed breed. Patricipation is a great way to meet other dog-lovers, socialize your dog to both other animals and people, enjoy the natural light your dog needs to stay healthy, have fun, and get exercise, all the while deepening your bond with your dog.

(Some) Sources Online
DownSouthWesties.com
MoonFruit.com
Westies-of-Yesteryear.co.uk
WestiezWinger.de
SouthernWestHighlandWhiteTerrierClub.uk
CoolDogBreeds.blogspot.com
AKC.org

(Some) Hard-copy Sources
Dogs and All About Them by Robert Leighton
Westies from Head to Tail by Ruth Faherty
The West Highland White Terrier by Rose Estes

The Author's Story

When our old dog Barleycorn (pictured in 2005), a Humane Society of Southern Arizona rescue mutt, died in 2009, we knew we'd want another dog someday.

We knew we'd want a smaller dog; Barley was medium-sized and weighed just over fifty pounds. We also agreed we wanted an up-eared dog, and one that was light-colored. Once we discovered the association of West Highland White Terriers – Westies – with our Scottish clan, the decision was made.

But ... would we look for a rescue or find a breeder? (Westie Rescue USA, sponsored by Westie Rescue of the MidAtlantic States, Inc., is one website where you can find connections to Westie rescue groups in many states.)

We went the purebred route for two reasons. One was that we wanted a puppy – so that in the beginning, the dog would be smaller than our old cats, and they'd have a chance to teach him that they were the alphas. The other was that we only wanted one dog, and while the adoption fee would help the Humane Society of Southern Arizona, if we went with a breeder we'd commit to making a more-than-one-dog donation to the HSSA.

We knew the best way to find a breeder was to attend dog shows and get recommendations from handlers, and meet breeders in person. We did that, and met and interviewed three breeders.

Inexperienced as we are with dog shows, we knew that the hour or so before a dog enters the ring is a busy time. Last minute grooming takes a lot of effort and attention. That's not the best time to talk at length with a breeder, but we wanted to introduce ourselves at that point in the process to see how the breeder handled the interruption. "Hi! This is a beautiful dog, and we're interested in a Westie. May we meet with you when you're done?" is what we said.

The first breeder we spoke to was very snappy. "I live in New Mexico," she said, and that was that. Never mind that she had come to Arizona for the show; her attitude was that it would be impossible for us to go to New Mexico to see her kennel and meet her dogs. Alrighty then!

The next breeder we met didn't seem upset that we wanted to talk briefly – but her handshake was almost imperceptible, and neither of us is comfortable with someone who lets the other person do all the work of shaking hands. We admired her dog, but we didn't ask to speak with her afterwards.

The third breeder was the charm. She had a firm handshake, and was happy to chat with us a little, even as she got her dog ready for the ring. We watched her show him, and she was confident and relaxed, as was her dog. As I recall, he won his ribbon (and by this time, may well have finished his championship).

We talked with her (Nancy Stolsmark of Headsup Westies - an AKC Breeder of Merit - see below) at some length after the show. We were in touch by e-mail for several weeks. She invited us to her home (where she has a room just for the dogs, and covered kennels taking up most of her yard) to meet a litter that was already spoken for, and get to know her and her dogs better.

She was planning to breed one of her bitches, and we agreed that we'd take one of Solo's pups. To be honest, we were hoping to get a girl, but Solo's first litter was small: there was one male and one female, and Nancy needed the female for her breeding program. We have the male.

Perhaps it is unusual for a breeder to keep in such close touch with the family that's taking one of her puppies, but Nancy sent us photos every week; sometimes there was a short video of the two pups. This let us feel that we'd known our puppy his whole life, and we cherish those "baby pictures."

We are grateful that some of those pictures included Drammy's only litter mate, Isla. When you read the update at the end of this section, you'll see why!

We spent hours thinking about our new dog's name, and finally settled on a registered name of Headsup Highland Adventure. His calling name is Wee Dram, and that's what's on his collar tag, but we mostly call him Dram or Drammy.

Our first dog, Barleycorn, was neutered before we brought him home from the Humane Society. However, we've agreed to leave Wee Dram intact for a few years – forever, if there are no medical issues – so that he can be available for stud.

Some of our friends ribbed us a little about that: "Oh, once he does *that*, he'll want to do *that* all the time," they warned us, with a bit of a chuckle. Well, just so you know, most breeders don't put two dogs in a room with a treat to share and romantic music in the background. For the male, it's a collection procedure, and for the female, it's artificial insemination.

Housetraining has kept indoor marking from being a problem, though during his puppyhood there were a few "excitement accidents." There is a risk of testicular cancer, but regular examination will reveal the swelling that's an early sign. We did a lot of research, and we're not worried about keeping Wee Dram intact.

We are being careful not to encourage what's called Small Dog Syndrome: we're training him not to jump on people unless he's invited (and now he usually stands on his hind legs a few inches away to see if he can get an invitation), and we don't let him put his teeth on us.

He has his own Facebook page: Wee Dram the Westie, - recently changed to Wee Dram the Westie and Sister Isla - so if you want to, you can follow his (their) adventures. I hope you've enjoyed "the Westie story," and that you'll take as much pride – and find as much joy - in the Clan MacCallum-Malcolm dogs as we do.

-- Ashleen O'Gaea
Tucson, Arizona, Winter 2014-15

Updates!

Some readers have said they wished this book was longer, and though we can't add much to the history of these wonderful little dogs, we can update you on our own experience.

Since we first published this book, Wee Dram – Headsup Highland Adventure – has earned his championship, so he's now CH Headsup Highland Adventure. We thank Lorainne Jardine, who with her husband John, is the owner of Dram's sire, for this photo of a photo of Dram's championship win.

As soon as he retired from the ring, we cut his hair, which makes camping (one of his favorite things) much easier for all of us. Here he is, all trimmed up so as not to collect sticks and burs when we go on lovely long walks. (Something quite close to the show stance is his default position. He's always ready for action!)

Not long after Drammy finished his championship., we found that we'd be adding his litter-mate twin sister Isla (pronounced eye-luh; Headsup Islay Single Malt is her formal name) would be joining our pack.

She's never been a show dog, so her coat's a little softer and she carries herself a little differently. She's a snuggle-bug, and her eagerness to cuddle has persuaded Dram that being a lap dog's not such a bad thing ....

Here are the two of them together – they're chair dogs, too, especially after one of us has made the chair's lap nice and warm.

Isla's first camping trip was in late August of 2016, and she took to it right away; here they are (Drammy on the left again) playing on the couch.

We are *all* still getting used to the brace coupler, but we got past the *get completely tangled up* stage in just a couple of days. (Dram's still on the left. I did indulge myself and got Isla a pink collar, and her individual leash is also pink.)

Here are pictures of Dram when he was a "baby puppy."

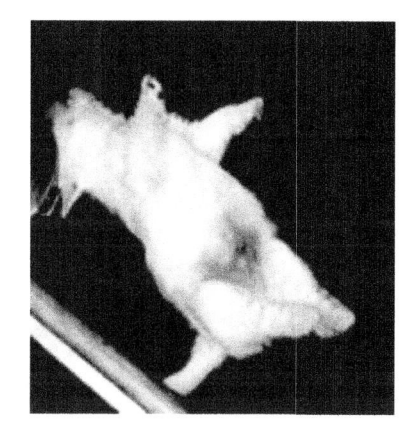

These eleven Poltalloch Terriers are among the first white dogs Malcolm bred. Given the opportunity, today's Westies will look just as rugged.

Below are a few more pictures of Dram and Isla when they were five or six weeks old. Sweet little things then, and sweet little things now.

You can meet Wee Dram (pictured here) and Isla, who will have her own tartan outfit, at Arizona Celtic Festivals where Clan MacCallum-Malcolm has a booth and dogs are allowed, and at the clan's booth at the Longs Peak Festival in Estes Park, Colorado. (Here, Dram's waiting for the 2014 Parade of the Tartans, which marches right through Estes Park, to begin.)

Going back to the source, let's close with a picture of Col. Malcolm with some of his dogs.

Half the proceeds from sales of this book go the MacCallum-Malcolm Clan Society of North America. You can find out more about this Scottish clan, or join – whether or not the name's in your family - at this website:

www.Clan-MacCallum-Malcolm.org

By the way, it doesn't matter how you spell the name. There are lots of variations; it's the consonants that matter, not the vowels!

CLAN MacCALLUM - MALCOLM SOCIETY
OF NORTH AMERICA, INC - A 501(c)(3) NOT FOR PROFIT CORPORATION

Robin Neill Lochnell Malcolm, Chief

New Member Application

Date: _____

To Neil McCallum, Sec./Treas. 2225 Keyes Ave., Madison, WI, 53711

I hereby apply for admission into membership of the Clan MacCallum-Malcolm Society of North America, Inc.

FULL NAME _____
(Please print)
SPOUSE'S NAME _____
CHILDREN'S NAME(S) & AGES _____

_____
HOME ADDRESS _____
TEL ( ) _____ EMAIL _____
CITY _____ STATE ___ ZIP _____
PLACE AND DATE OF BIRTH _____
SCOTTISH BIRTH/DESCENT/SCOTTISH ANCESTOR (if any)

_____

SIGNATURE _____

The purposes of this Society shall be: A). to promote the preservation and study of Scottish history, culture and heritage; B). the acquisition, compilation, preservation and distribution of information of historical, cultural and genealogical interest to those of the surname, MacCallum, McCallum, McCollum, Malcolm and its families, regardless of spelling; C). to provide for the public a forum for discussion groups, lectures, musical programs, entertainment and instruction on our Scottish cultural heritage; D). to cooperate with other Scottish Clan and Celtic organizations that have like interests; and E). to disseminate information of an advisory and educational nature which will be of value to its members and the general public.

Annual Dues: __ 1 year for $25; __ 2 years for $50; __ 3 years for $75; or __ years at $25/year$_____

Please make checks payable to Clan MacCallum-Malcolm Society of North America, Inc.

FOR CLAN MACCALLUM-MALCOLM USE ONLY
DUES PAID $ _____ Number of years _____ ___ cash ___ check
Games location _____
Date _____ Received by _____